CONTENTS

MEMO

FROM: Judge Talon
TO: All Tomb Guards
SUBJECT: Thefts from Royal Tombs

This is getting worse every year and Pharaoh is very concerned. We have got to catch more robbers and make an example of them. We will show no mercy. After considering many types of punishment –

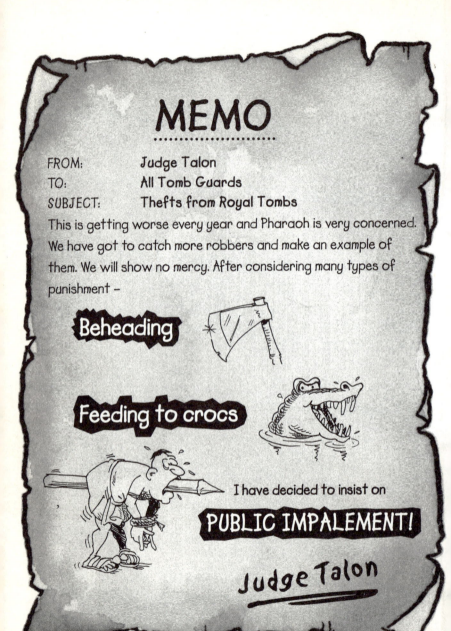

Beheading

Feeding to crocs

I have decided to insist on

PUBLIC IMPALEMENT!

Judge Talon

4

"I know what we'll do," said Dad.

He frowned at the mangy lion in its small cage on the deck. It was all they'd got left to trade, and what was it worth?

Not much.

"Ptoni can train that lion to jump through a flaming hoop – and you can help him, Stupor." Dad aimed a kick at the sleeping scribe. "Then we'll put on a show, draw the crowds and make a quick fortune. Then I could exchange *Hefijuti* for a much bigger boat – and be a rich merchant, like Kashpot!"

His crew swapped sullen glances.

"If that's the best you can offer, chief . . ."

"When we haven't been paid for months, then . . ."

"It's time we went our own way."

One of the lads twisted the steering oar.

"Where are you going?" Dad blustered.

The lads didn't bother to answer. Instead they aimed *Hefijuti* towards the nearest bank, and as the boat ploughed into the rushes, all three jumped over the side.

"We've got to get proper jobs, chief."
"From someone who'll pay us real wages."
"Cheerio, skipper."

"Ungrateful fools!" Dad shouted as the lads padded off up a track towards the nearest village, with Stupor puffing behind them. "Stupor, you can't go with them. Come back. You're my personal scribe. Oh, what have I done to deserve this?"

The lion roared with hunger.

"Oh, shut up," said Dad. "Hey Ptoni,

if we cover his cage, he'll think it's time for bed, and go to sleep and stop roaring."

Ptoni helped him unfurl the spare sail, and drape it over the lion's cage. "But maybe the lads are right, Dad. We all ought to get proper jobs."

Dad looked stunned. "I'm a trader! We just need to find some new crewmen. I'll get some in the next village."

They trudged along the river bank towards the nearest houses.

On the left was a run-down tavern, where
Stupor was quenching his thirst.

Behind the tavern were a couple of
workshops with painted signs over their doors.

Then Ptoni noticed three shifty men
coming out of the shade of some palm trees.

"Perhaps we'd better back off, Dad,"
said Ptoni. "They look like robbers."

But Dad strolled up to them. "Evening all! How would you good fellows fancy a life on the river, manning my trading ship?"

The good fellows gathered round. They were an ugly bunch. The one with the eye patch did the talking.

"I'm Armpit. This is Hack, and here's my best mate, Razor."

Razor looked smooth but sharp. Hack was jagged and jumpy, with a bandage wrapped round the top of his head.

"How nice to meet you," said Dad.

Armpit grinned down at Dad. "It's more than nice – it's lucky. We've been looking out for a handy boat like yours to pick up some cargo for us. It could be a nice little earner."

"We're ready when you are," Dad grinned back. "Just find the lads, will you, Ptoni?"

Armpit gripped Dad's arm. "Nah, skipper. We'll help with the boat. Then you won't have to pay wages."

Dad nodded with approval. "I can tell you've a good head for business. Just like me. We'll be ready to set off first thing in the morning!"

"Nah. We'll go tonight. As soon as it gets dark, skip!"

Ptoni didn't like this one bit. He tried to nudge Dad in the ribs. But Dad led the way to the boat, boasting about all the cargoes he'd shifted over the years, and all the great deals he'd done. "I even traded a whole load of rot-gut wine to the Palace, and Pharaoh liked it so much he made me a tax collector."

"*Pharaoh made you a tax collector?*"

"Well . . . just for a day," said Dad.

His new chums admired *Hefijuti*.

"What's that sheet of canvas?"

"Oh, that's for cargo," replied Dad. "To keep it well-covered in transit."

"Now that's very shrewd," agreed Armpit. "We don't want any prying eyes on this trip – so that's where we'll hide *our* cargo."

"Er, what is your cargo?" asked Ptoni.

"Ptoni," cried Dad. "Mind your manners."

"That's right." Armpit winked at Ptoni. "If you don't ask any questions, I won't have to tell you any lies."

Razor and Hack both laughed.

It was a nasty noise.

"But it's our boat," said Ptoni, "and as we're coming on this voyage, we'll see what you've got."

"You won't," Armpit said. "It'll be in big sacks. But seeing as we'll be ship-mates, I'll let you into the secret – it's *extremely valuable clay*."

"What do you want valuable clay for?"

"Shard's Pottery wants it, young sir. This clay is sacred clay. Shard needs it to make sacred pots.* And there's only one place to get sacred clay, and that's from a sacred clay pit."

"How interesting," said Dad brightly.

"But there's a catch," said Armpit. "The only sacred clay pit is under one of those pyramids you can see in the distance." He pointed down the river. "That's why we've got to go at night, see? Trespassers aren't very welcome."

* A potter could earn a good living – see page 60.

For the first time Dad looked worried.
"Nah, nah," said Armpit. "No problems.
I'm best friends with all the guards!"

CHAPTER 3
DAD SEES AN OPENING

There were plenty of problems, setting sail with three useless strangers instead of the lads as crewmen. Ptoni did all the work.

First he had to put the sail up.

Then he had to dangle a lantern over the prow so that he could check that there weren't any sand banks.

"The moon's coming up," said Armpit. "We'll pass Tutinkarhorn's Pyramid first.*"

* Find out more about pyramids on page 61

"Then it's King Milksop's," said Hack.

"And then it's the Pointless one. That's where we moor the boat."

"What's pointless about it?" asked Dad.

"The top bit must have been built on the cheap. It caved in, didn't it, skip?"

"I still don't get it," said Dad.

"Why don't they repair it?" asked Ptoni.

"Can't be bothered," said Armpit. "Let's face it, who cares about pyramids these days?

The nobs all want underground tombs."

"And lucky for us," said Razor. "We can just take what we find."

"Clay," added Armpit quickly.

"Yes, but why call the pyramid pointless?" Dad asked again.

Nobody bothered to answer.

In silence they drifted downstream, and nudged the boat into some rushes. Razor and Hack jumped ashore.

"That's it," said Armpit softly. "Now wait here until we come back, skip. But don't make any noise."

As soon as the gang had slunk off, Dad said at the top of his voice, "I think we've done pretty well, teaming up with Armpit. We'll ask for a cut of his sacred clay. Then we can push off up river. We'll call at all the big potteries and drum up some orders, Ptoni.

Then we'll come back here and help ourselves. Armpit's setting his sights too low, just getting the clay for old Shard."

"But what are we going to do now, Dad?"

Dad looked at the lion's covered cage. "Let's row across to the other bank and say goodbye to that cat."

Ptiddles was upset.

"I didn't mean you, Ptiddles, you silly cat. I meant the lion."

Ptiddles started purring.

"Right Ptoni, jump over the side and give *Hefijuti* a push."

"Hold on a minute, Dad."

"Not scared of crocodiles, are you?"

Ptoni had been doing some thinking.

What sort of sacred clay pit would be under a pyramid?

And what *was* sacred clay?

He had a nasty suspicion that Armpit had set his sights on things of much higher value than even Dad had imagined.

But knowing that Dad wouldn't believe this, Ptoni said, "If we're going to come back and pick up more sacred clay, we'll need to know where to find it."

"Armpit said under the pyramid."

"A pyramid's quite a big thing, Dad."

There was a long silence.

"Perhaps we should check," said Dad.

Dad led the way, with Ptoni close behind him holding the oil lamp. Before long they reached the edge of a clearing. Some guards were sprawled beside a fire, passing round a large wine pot.

"We should have brought Stupor," said Dad. "They look a friendly lot. Let's go and say hello and tell them we're friends with Armpit."

"Sssh! Safer to avoid them and skirt round the edge."

They reached the base of the pyramid and started the long walk round it. But halfway along the first side, Ptoni saw what looked like an entrance – a small oblong hole in the stone work.

"What's this?" He picked up one end of a length of yellow thread. It trailed away down some steps into the bowels of the pyramid. "Armpit must have left this to help him find his way out!"

"Armpit's not stupid," said Dad. "Perhaps I should make him my partner."

Setting off down the steps they soon found themselves in a corridor which carried on down a slope. At the bottom it forked. The yellow thread lead to the left. So they followed it down into another passage. This one had such a low ceiling Dad had to walk with his head bowed.

"This place is a maze," said Dad. "No wonder the clay's worth a fortune."

Ptoni whispered to Dad to be quiet. From some way off he heard voices. Peering round the next corner he saw a light up ahead. He decided to blow out his own lamp.

In the darkness he heard Armpit laughing.

"If only that fool of a boatman could see all our *sacred clay*!"

"His eyes would pop out of his stupid head, boss!"

"Valuable clay! Tee-hee!"

Ptoni couldn't stop Dad from pushing past to get a closer look.

Then, craning his neck round the doorway, Dad leant out a bit too far.

"Owweee!" He lost his balance and went stumbling into the chamber.

Ptoni heard clangs and clatter. It sounded as if lots of metal objects were being bashed into each other. Then Razor and Hack were shouting, and Dad was yelping and gasping.

Ptoni got to the doorway in time to see Dad on the floor, with Razor and Hack on his back. Armpit was on the far side, with his hands in an open casket. He was helping himself to the gold mask that had covered the face of the mummy. It was studded with valuable jewels like amethysts and turquoises.*

* Egyptians loved jewels – see page 62

"So, where's the boy?" asked Armpit.

Ptoni dodged back out of sight. He flattened himself in a niche and waited, holding his breath.

"No sign of him here," said Razor, peering out of the doorway.

"That's good. We'll pick him up later after we sort out this treasure."

"So we just have to sort his Dad out now?"

"Let me give him the chop," offered Hack.

"Nah. Put him in with the mummy. He'll keep her company, won't he?"

"HA! HA! HA! HA! HA!"

Ptoni heard Dad put up a noisy struggle – yelling, shrieking and pleading.

But suddenly –

CLONK!

Then silence.

"Let's go," said Armpit calmly.

CHAPTER 5
DON'T LOSE THE THREAD

As soon as the robbers had gone, taking their oil lamp with them, Ptoni stepped out of the niche. He groped his way back to the doorway and shuffled into the burial chamber.

"Dad?" he called softly.

Silence.

"CAN YOU HEAR ME, DAD?"

Ptoni made out a faint muffled sound.

"Get me . . . out of . . . here!"

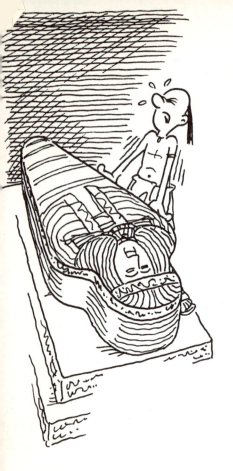

It was Dad's voice, and it came from inside the mummy's casket!

Ptoni's fingers brushed over the casket. It was chiselled from solid stone. He tried to lift the lid, but it was much too heavy.

"I'm sorry, Dad, I'll have to get help."

That was easier said than done. Stumbling about in the darkness Ptoni kept bumping into the walls. Then he remembered the yellow thread. If only Armpit had left it!

He sank to his hands and knees. The stone floor had gritty bits on it that grazed his knees. He was sweating, but he was shivering too. Then his fingers touched something stringy.

Phew!

Ptoni started to shuffle along, playing the thread through his hands, doing his best not to think about Dad being cooped up with that mummy.

He stood up and made better progress. He hurried along the passage and climbed the flight of stairs. At last Ptoni saw light up ahead. He stepped into the warm friendly night. The guards were still by the campfire.

"Excuse me."

The guards looked up. They were old men.

And when Ptoni tried to explain the situation, they weren't very quick on the uptake.

"Did you say pyramid?"

"Which one?"

"The pointless one!" cried Ptoni. "The one you're supposed to be guarding!"

"You're not allowed to go in there. You could have got lost," said the oldest guard.

"The robbers put down a length of thread."

"What robbers? We've been here all evening."

"You were drinking," shouted Ptoni. "And now the robbers are going to escape with their loot on my Dad's boat!"

The Head Guard yawned. But, as all the other guards yawned too, there was a mighty ROAR!

"What's that?"

"That's a lion," said Ptoni.

The guards all struggled to get up,

but they were still on their knees as Armpit,
Hack and Razor came sprinting up the track,
lugging their sacks.

"That's them! Those are the thieves!"
Ptoni cried.

The guards grabbed their spears and went
hobbling after them. All except the Head
Guard, who needed help to stand.

He gripped Ptoni's wrist. "Not so fast. At
least I've caught one of the gang. You're
coming with me – to the Guard House!"

"But I'm not a thief," cried Ptoni.

"We'll see about that in the morning."

"What's special about the morning?"

"You won't see a better one, sonny. Not if you're sentenced to death."

It was quite late in the morning when the Head Guard opened the cell door.

"You're wanted – by Judge Talon."

"But what about all the others?"

"The rest of your crew got away. However, we caught the lion, and Judge Talon fancies adding a lion to his private zoo. So that might count in your favour."

"What about my Dad?"

"The weedy chap who got into Queen Hedbutt's casket? He's committed sacrilege. He's in *real* trouble."

Judge Talon looked like a vulture. He had

a hooked nose and sharp eyes. He was showing a scroll to some other official as Ptoni was dragged into the room. He looked up. "Is that the scum?"

"No, your Eminence. This is just the scum's son. I'll fetch the scum now if you like."

"Like?" snapped the judge. "I've been sent here by Chief Counsellor Donut to mount a full enquiry. There's hardly a tomb on this sacred site that hasn't been broken into. And now this wretch has . . ."

He paused for breath as Dad was led into the yard by two of the elderly guards.

"I ask you, is NOTHING sacred?"

Dad put his hand up.

"What is it?" snarled the judge.

Ptoni feared that Dad was going to say 'sacred clay' but Dad had other ideas.

"May I ask if there's a reward, sire?"

"Why do you want to know?"

"I know the culprit. His name is Armpit, your Scribeship."

"*You're* an armpit!" the judge roared. "And what's more, you'll be punished!"

"But I've already been punished. I was stuck in a box all night on top of a shrivelled old mummy! I'm only an innocent trader."

"Then why has your boat been rigged up with a covered compartment for stealing stolen treasure?"

"No, no," Dad held up his hands. "That's just a home for our pet lion. My son wants to teach him new tricks. Though if you'd like a pet lion in exchange for . . ."

"Pet?" rapped the judge. "That lion is wild and untamed. He scared off your cowardly gang. But enough about lions. I want to know who's behind this tomb robbery. There's always some big wheeler-dealer who handles stolen treasures."

Dad grinned. "Yes. Probably Kashpot."

Judge Talon looked at him coldly. "Kashpot is a very important merchant. You'll have to do better than that. Or I shall pass sentence. You'll get the usual treatment reserved for vermin who rob royal tombs.*"

Dad blinked at him in amazement. "What is the usual treatment?"

Judge Talon simply pointed to one of the older guards who seemed to be propping himself up with help from two wooden stakes. Ptoni noticed they had sharpened ends. Then he noticed another old guard was holding a hefty hammer.

"Impalement?" Dad went pale.

* Tomb robbers were dealt with harshly – see page 63

"What does that mean?" Ptoni gulped.

"It means we skewer you – like a kebab!" said the judge. "In one end. Out the other."

It wasn't a pleasant thought.

"Entirely your choice," the judge added. "I'm going to count from twenty to give you time to tell me where the treasure's been taken.

Fair enough? Nineteen. Eighteen."

Ptoni's mind had gone blank.

"No," Dad protested. "It's not fair. I only came for the clay!"

"Fifteen. Fourteen."

"No, please. I was misguided by Armpit."

"Thirteen. Twelve. Eleven."

"Armpit said he was friends with the guards."

"Ten."

The guard swung his hammer.

"Nine."

"He said we were only here to pick up some sacred clay."

"Eight."

"From the sacred clay pits."

"Seven."

"To make sacred pots."

"Six."

"But it's true," cried Ptoni. "Dad's not guilty. He's just stupid. But Armpit and his two helpers have got . . ."

"Five."

"Five sacks of treasure."

"Four."

"For Shard the Potter."

"Why would he want treasure? Three. Two."

"To melt it down and sell . . . to . . . er. . . Nugget the Jeweller."

"One," said Talon calmly, "has to explore all the options. We'd better check up on Shard."

CHAPTER 7
SACRED CLAY SACKS

The guards marched Ptoni and Dad down to a landing stage where Judge Talon's galley was waiting to whisk them back up the river.

As they sped past *Hefijuti*, King Milksop's Pyramid and finally, the grand Pyramid of Tutinkarhorn, Dad was whistling brightly. But Ptoni was still very worried. They only had Armpit's word that Shard had sent them down river to pick up "sacred clay".

And could Armpit be trusted?

Of course not!

By the time they reached the village, the sun was scorching the earth and the whole world seemed to be sleeping.

Stupor was outside the tavern, flat on his back, and three figures were sitting with their backs to the wall, next to the pottery door.

"Hi, chief!"

"Hi, skipper."

"Hi, captain."

"It's the lads," cried Dad. "Now these are my *real* crewmen."

"Arrest them," ordered Talon.

The guards grabbed hold of the lads, while the judge thumped the door with his stick.

At last a small man with a hot sweaty face opened the door of the pottery. He was backed by three bigger men.

Armpit, Razor and Hack!

"See! *Those* are the robbers," cried Ptoni.

"What's this?" said Shard. "We're busy. We're firing pots in the kiln."

"Not sacred pots?" Dad called out. "Not made with sacred clay?"

"Are you mocking my work?" Shard demanded.

"What work?" asked Dad. "Go on, tell us!"

"This man has got sun stroke," snapped Shard.

"More like mummy stroke," said the Head Guard. "But step aside please. Quickly. Let my men in."

"Every minute is precious," said Shard.

The guards went through the pottery, searching high and low. But they didn't find any treasure.

So then they searched everybody.
They searched Hack, Armpit and Razor.
They even looked under Shard's loin cloth.
And lastly they searched the lads.
"Ah ha," cried the guard with the last lad.
"Look at this!" He held up a large amethyst.
"You've got the thieves!" Shard shouted,

hopping about. "Now get out and leave at once. Our pots will be over-baked. Quick!"

But Ptoni fell on his knees and clutched Talon's bony ankles. "Please, sire, the guard must have planted that gem."

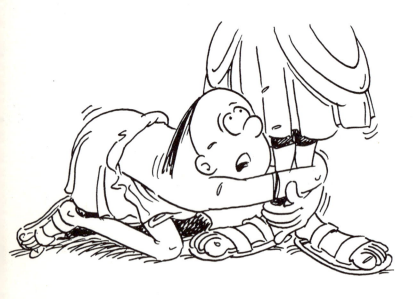

"No he didn't," the lad said. "I found it."

"And where would scum like you find a gem like this?" asked the judge. "It was prized off Queen Hedbutt's death mask."

"We came to this pot shop asking for work, sire. This bloke," the lad pointed at Armpit, "was lugging in sacks of clay and the gem tumbled out. So I swiped it. I mean to say, finder's keepers."

"So where is the rest of the treasure?"

Shard glanced at the kiln. He looked desperate.

And suddenly Ptoni guessed why. They were melting down the stolen treasure!

Dodging between Shard and Armpit, he unplugged the mouth of the kiln and a great wave of heat gusted out.

"You'll ruin my pots!" screeched Shard.

But as the smoke cleared away and everyone peered in the kiln, it was clear they were ruined already.

There was nothing in there but a puddle of gold, dotted with sparkly stones.

"Well I don't know," said Dad after Shard and his helpers had been arrested and led off to board the galley. "Talon could have had the decency to offer us a lift. After all, we solved that mystery for him. I've a good mind to go and tell Pharaoh."

"At least we weren't kebabbed, Dad."

"And we've got the gem," grinned Dad, darting a glance at one of the lads who was cradling it in his hands. "That judge was a fool to forget that."

He grabbed it.

"Oy, chief . . ."

"That's ours . . ."

"We found it . . ."

"And we're going to share it," said Dad. "As an experienced trader, I'll know the best place to trade it. And then I might pay you your wages."

"But that's not fair!"

"Who says life is fair? Was it fair I was buried alive while you were all drinking with Stupor?"

"Oh yeah?"

"Pull the other one, chief!"

"Go on. Tell us where you went last night."

Ptoni took a deep breath. There were so many things he could tell them about Dad's lucky escape, but what was the point?

Dad pointed to the Pointless Pyramid. "That's where I spent the night, lads. I had to get quite close to Queen Hedbutt in order to catch those rogues. But now the tomb's been

robbed, so there's nothing inside except a few bones and some bandages. It's just a big pointless heap of old stones. Though come to think of it, Ptoni, if I trade this gem for a much bigger boat we could go into the stone trade. We'll find someone building a palace and . . ."

"You'd better get back to the point, Dad."

"Ah yes, the point," Dad droned on. He was looking a little bit woozy after his night with Queen Hedbutt. "What is the point? I've forgotten."

"The pyramid," said Ptoni.

"That's it," said Dad. "Except that –"
He broke off, cupped his hands over his eyes and peered down the river. His face lit up. "I've got it! The reason it's called that is because it's not got any point! And that's why it's known to those in the know as . . ."

Potters

Skilled craftsmen were always in demand in Ancient Egypt. A good potter could make an excellent living because people needed lots of pots. Storage jars, jugs, lamps, cooking pots and many different kinds of serving vessels were all produced by potters.

Pyramids

Pyramids were massive mountains of stone built to house the tombs of early pharaohs.

They were not built by slaves, but by ordinary farmers, working during the time their fields were flooded by the Nile. Thousands of men worked in teams to build the pyramids. They dragged blocks of stones up a mud and brick ramp. The ramp was made higher and higher as the pyramid grew layer by layer. When all the layers were in place, the topmost stone was added and the ramp was dismantled.

Jewels

Egyptians enjoyed wearing jewellery and markets sold gleaming necklaces, bracelets and rings made from coloured glass. Wealthy people wore gold ornaments. The gold was obtained from the desert, as were jewels such as cornelian and amethysts. Turquoises came from Sinai which belonged to Egypt. Other jewels, such as the rich blue lapis lazuli, were imported from as far away as Afghanistan.

Tomb robbers

A pharaoh's tomb was filled with costly objects which he might need in the After Life. This posed a security problem, because robbers broke into the tombs to steal the treasures. Robbers were dealt with severely and impalement was just one of several horrible punishments doled out to them.

Join Ptoni and his Dad up the Nile
in these other books.

THE SCRUNCHY SCARAB

0 7496 3649 1 (Hbk)   0 7496 3653 X (Pbk)

The town of Feruka is having a big celebration, but all Dad has to sell are some dried-up figs and a few old flasks of oil. Fortunately Ptoni finds a lucky scarab beetle – so perhaps things will change for the better?

THE MISSING MUMMY

0 7496 3650 X (Hbk)   0 7496 3654 6 (Pbk)

Dad goes to collect some wine he is owed by Slosh, the merchant. But poor Slosh has died, and someone has stolen his mummy. It's up to Ptoni to find it, and to claim the wine.

THE FEARFUL PHARAOH

0 7496 3651 3 (Hbk)   0 7496 3655 6 (Pbk)

Pharaoh Armenlegup is having a big festival to celebrate his long reign. So everybody is happy – everybody, that is, except Dad. He's been sentenced to death!

THE HELPFUL HIEROGLYPH

0 7496 3652 1 (Hbk)   0 7496 3656 4 (Pbk)

Pharaoh has ordered Dad to pick up some taxes for him – but Dad can't read. So he hires an old scribe to teach Ptoni how to understand the hieroglyphs. It's a harder job than they thought!

THE JINXED SPHINX

0 7496 3987 3 (Hbk)   0 7496 4021 9 (Pbk)

All Dad has to trade is a sphinx with a chip on its shoulder. But the three dancing girls who hitch a lift on his boat think they can help. They only make the situation worse!